PENROD'S PICTURE

Mary Blount Christian

Pictures by S. D. Schindler

Ready-to-Read®

Macmillan Publishing Company   New York
Collier Macmillan Canada   Toronto
Maxwell Macmillan International Publishing Group
New York   Oxford   Singapore   Sydney

To Maggie—
so glad you're part
of our family now

Text copyright © 1991 by Mary Blount Christian
Illustrations copyright © 1991 by S. D. Schindler
All rights reserved. No part of this book may be reproduced
or transmitted in any form or by any means, electronic or mechanical,
including photocopying, recording, or any information storage and
retrieval system, without permission in writing from the Publisher.
Macmillan Publishing Company
866 Third Avenue, New York, NY 10022
Collier Macmillan Canada, Inc.
1200 Eglinton Avenue East, Suite 200
Don Mills, Ontario M3C 3N1
First edition
Printed in Hong Kong by South China Printing Company (1988) Ltd.
1 2 3 4 5 6 7 8 9 10
The text of this book is set in 18 point Century Expanded.
The illustrations are rendered in gouache and watercolor.
READY-TO-READ is a registered trademark of Macmillan, Inc.

Library of Congress Cataloging-in-Publication Data
Christian, Mary Blount.
Penrod's picture / Mary Blount Christian ; pictures by S.D.
Schindler. — 1st ed.
p.   cm. — (Ready-to-read)
Summary: Follows the humorous antics of Penrod Porcupine and
Griswold Bear as they hang a picture, go camping, plant a garden,
and have a garage sale.
ISBN 0-02-718523-0
[1. Porcupines—Fiction. 2. Bears—Fiction. 3. Friendship—
Fiction.] I. Schindler, S. D., ill. II. Title. III. Series.
PZ7.C4528Pg 1991   [E]—dc20   90-39808

p^3

CONTENTS

PENROD'S PICTURE

Penrod Porcupine hurried
to Griswold Bear's house.
He wanted to show his friend
the picture
he had painted.

"Ummmm," Griswold said.
"What a nice picture
of a potato."

"No," Penrod said.
"It goes *this* way."

"Oh!" Griswold said.
"That is better!
    What a nice picture
    of a tree!"

"It is not a tree,"
    Penrod said.
"And it is not a potato.
    It is me!"

Griswold turned the picture
this way and that.
He turned his head
this way and that.
"Of course!" he said.
"Now I see.
Those aren't tree limbs.
Those are your quills.
What a lovely picture.
Why, anyone would be *proud*
to have that picture."

Penrod smiled at Griswold.
"It is my best picture.
  And you are my best friend.
  You should have it."

"No, no!" Griswold said.
"I could not take
  your best picture."

"It will be perfect
  in your living room,"
  Penrod said.
"Everyone will see it there."

Griswold frowned.
"Yes, they will."

"All we need is the hammer
and a nail," Penrod said.

"I do not know where they are,"
Griswold said.

"I do," Penrod said.
He found the hammer and a nail.

Griswold groaned.
"I will hang it myself,"
he said.

Tappity tap tap.
The hammer hit the nail.
Tappity tap tap thump!
The hammer hit Griswold's thumb!
"Ouch!" Griswold yelled.
"Oh, oh, oh!"

"Oh, dear," Penrod said.

"You must soak your thumb
in cold water.
I will hang the picture
for you."

"That is what I am afraid of,"
Griswold mumbled.
He went to soak his thumb.

Tappity tap tap.
Penrod hit the nail
with the hammer.
Tappity tap tap thump!
The hammer hit the wall.
A long crack ripped
across the wall.
"Oops," Penrod said.

"Why did you say 'Oops'?"
Griswold called.

"Do not worry!"
Penrod said.
He hammered some more.
Tappity tap tap thump!
A chunk of the wall fell down.
"Oops!" Penrod said.

"What?" Griswold called.
"Did you say 'Oops' again?"

"Do not worry!" Penrod said.
He hammered some more.
Tappity tap tap thump!
This time a *huge* chunk
fell from the wall.
Penrod could see outside.
"Oooooh," Penrod said.

"Why did you say 'Oooooh'?"
Griswold called.

"Do not worry!"
Penrod called back.

"I *am* worried!" Griswold said.
"I am *very* worried!"

Penrod hurried outside
to gather the chunks of wall.
He heard Griswold coming.
He peeked through the hole.

"This is amazing!"
Griswold said.
"Now that the picture
is on the wall,
it looks just like Penrod!"

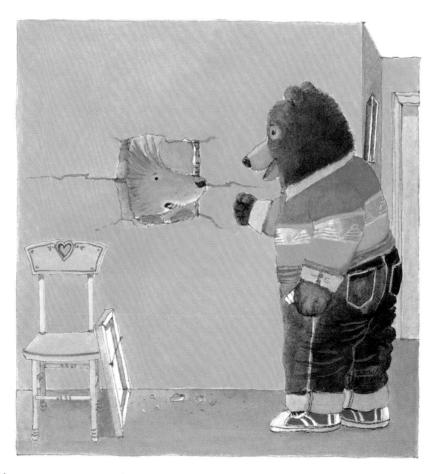

"That is because
  it *is* me!" Penrod said.

"Oooooh," Griswold said.

"Dear Griswold," Penrod said.
"I did not mean
  to make a hole
  in your wall.
  It is good that
  you have my picture
  to cover it."

Grrrrr! Griswold said.

PENROD'S ALMANAC

Griswold's Aunt Bruin
gave him money
to buy camping gear.
Penrod went with his friend
to the shopping mall.

"Oh," Penrod said,
"we will need
a *Farmer's Almanac*.
It will tell us
the perfect day for camping."

"Very well," said Griswold.
"You buy it.
Here is some money."

Penrod and Griswold
met later.
"I bought a bedroll,
a picnic basket,
and a cook pot," Griswold said.
"I can hardly wait
to go camping!"

"I bought the *Farmer's Almanac*,"
Penrod said.
"It is just like the one
Grandpa Bristles has.
But it was half the price.
It was on sale."
He gave Griswold the change.

Penrod looked in the book.
"Tomorrow will be
a perfect day
for camping," he said.

Penrod and Griswold stopped
at the grocer's.
They bought wieners and buns.

Early the next morning,
Penrod packed pickles
and mustard in a sack.
He packed potato chips
and sodas, too.
He carried the almanac.

Griswold was waiting for him.

"The sky is gray,"
he said.

"Maybe we should not
go camping today."

"Do not worry,"
Penrod said.

"The almanac says
blue skies today."

Rrrrrumble!

"That sounded like thunder,"
Griswold said.
"Maybe it will rain.
We should not
go camping today."

"That could not be thunder,"
Penrod said.
"The almanac says
sunny and hot.
Today is a perfect day
for camping."

They pedaled to the edge
of the woods.
Then they walked their bikes
down the trail.

Griswold looked up.

"It is getting dark," he said.

"It is going to rain.
   We should go home."

Penrod laughed.

"It is not going to rain.
   The almanac says blue skies.
   It says sunny and hot.
   Today is a perfect day
   for camping."

"There!" Griswold said.
"That is a good place to camp."
He gathered wood
for a campfire.
He lit the wood.

Splish!
"I felt a raindrop!"
he said.
Splish splash!
"I felt *two* raindrops!"

Penrod took the buns
and wieners from the sack.
"That could not be rain,"
he said.
"The almanac says blue skies.
It says sunny and hot."

Splish splish splish splash!
More drops fell.
Sizzle!
The campfire went out.

"I know rain when it hits me,"
Griswold said.
"It *is* raining!"

Splish splish splish splash!
Rumble rumble boom!
The two friends
held Griswold's bedroll
over their heads.
The rain beat against it.

Rivulets washed past them.
The buns grew soggy.
The wieners floated away.

"You and your dumb almanac!"
Griswold grumbled.
"It does not know a sunny day
from a rainy one."

Penrod shrugged.
"It always works
   for Grandpa Bristles."

Griswold grabbed the almanac.
"Penrod!" he said.
"This almanac
   is from *last* year!"

"Oh, no," Penrod said.
"That must be why
   it was half price."

Grrrrr!

GRISWOLD'S GARDEN

Griswold pointed to the holes
he had dug.
"I will plant
these little seeds,"
he told Penrod.
"Soon I will have carrots,
peas, lettuce,
and green beans."

Griswold's phone rang.
He went to answer it.
He came back and said,
"That was Grandma Griselda.
She has the flu.
I will go to her house
and take care of her.
I will have to seed
my garden later."

"How do you seed
a garden?" Penrod asked.

"You put the seeds
into the holes,"
Griswold said.
"Then you cover them
with a little dirt."

"I will seed your garden,"
Penrod said.

Griswold groaned.

"Do not worry," Penrod said.

"I will call you
from Grandma Griselda's,"
Griswold promised.

After Griswold left,
Penrod put the seeds
into the holes.
"That was easy!"
he said.
He put away the tools
and went home.

The phone rang.

It was Griswold.

"Grandma Griselda
is better.
I will stay here
until she is well.
Did you seed my garden?"

"Yes," Penrod said.
"Do not worry."

"Did you *water* the seeds?"
Griswold asked.

"Water?" Penrod asked.

"You must water the seeds
to make them grow,"
Griswold told him.

The next day,
Penrod watered the garden.
"If a little water is good,
a lot of water is better,"
he said.
He watered some more.

Soon water was everywhere.
It floated under the fence
and into Penrod's yard.
He went home.

Griswold called again.
"Did you water the garden?"
he asked Penrod.

"Yes," Penrod said.
"Do not worry."

"Did you *weed* the garden?"

"Oops!" Penrod said.
"I will weed it tomorrow."

Penrod thought and thought.
He had seeded the garden
by putting seeds in it.
He had watered the garden
by putting water on it.
So to *weed* the garden,
he must put weeds in it.
Penrod went to
Sam Spoonbill's nursery.

"We have everything
for the garden,"
Sam Spoonbill told him.

"Do you have any weeds?"
Penrod asked.

"Certainly not!"
Sam Spoonbill said.

"Then you don't have *everything* for the garden," Penrod said.

Penrod saw Rhoda Horse.
"Where can I get some weeds?"
he asked her.

Rhoda laughed.
"You can have mine!"
she said.

Penrod went to Rhoda's house.
She pointed out the weeds.
Penrod dug them up.
He carried them to Griswold's.
Carefully,
Penrod planted the weeds.
They grew and grew.

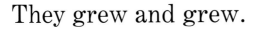

At last,
Grandma Griselda got well.
Griswold came home.
He went to look
at his garden.
"What happened?"
he yelled.
"Why are all these weeds
in my garden?"

"You told me
  to seed your garden,"
  Penrod said.
"I put in the seeds.
  You told me to water
  your garden.
  I put water on it.
  Then you told me
  to weed your garden.
  So I put weeds in it."

Griswold looked closer.
"Where are my veggies?"

Penrod shrugged.
"I planted them."

Griswold pointed
to the pictures
on the seed packages.
"Do you see anything here
that looks like these?"

"Oooooh," Penrod said.
"I know where they are!"
He pointed to his own yard.
"The seeds must have floated over
when I watered," he said.

Griswold rumbled
deep in his throat.

"Do not worry," Penrod said.
"When the vegetables are ready,
I will invite you to my house
for a fresh garden salad."

Grrrrr!

GARAGE SALE

"I am so tired
  of my furniture,"
  Griswold grumbled.
"My house is boring!"

"Mine, too!" Penrod said.
"Why don't we have
  a garage sale?
  We can sell our old stuff.
  Then we can buy new stuff."

"We can hang signs
  around town," Griswold said.
"We can put an ad
  in the newspaper."

Penrod made
some signs.

> Our junk may be
> your treasure
> Penrod and Griswold's
> garage sale
> This Saturday
> In Griswold's garage

Tappity tap tap.
They hung the signs
all over town.

They moved Griswold's
old green couch
to his garage.
Then they moved Penrod's
rosy pink couch
to the garage.

Griswold put his green lamp
in the garage.
Penrod put his pink lamp
in the garage.

Griswold put his green rug
in the garage.
Penrod put his pink rug
in the garage.

They put in dishes and vases
and pitchers and glasses.
They put in throw pillows, too.
Soon Griswold's garage
was filled with their things.

"I have always liked
  that green couch,"
  Penrod told Griswold.
"I think I will buy it."

"To tell you the truth,"
  Griswold said,
"I like your pink one better."

"Why don't we trade?"
  Penrod asked.

They put the green couch
in Penrod's house.
They put the pink couch
in Griswold's house.

"Now that I have
   a green couch,"
   Penrod said,
"I could use that green lamp."

"And that pink lamp
   would go nicely with *my* couch,"
   Griswold said.
   They traded lamps.

They traded rugs.
They traded dishes and vases
and pitchers and glasses.
They traded throw pillows, too.

There was nothing left
for the garage sale.
They took down the signs
all over town.

"That was a lot of work,"
Penrod said.
"I think we should have
some lemonade."

Griswold made some lemonade.
He poured it from
his new pink pitcher
into his new pink glasses.
They sat on his new pink couch.

Penrod took a sip.
"You know, Griswold," he said,
"I have always felt
at home here.
But now I am really comfortable
at your house."

Griswold laughed.
"I think I will feel
the same way
at your house."